For my children,

George and Matilda,

who fill my (once quiet) life

with a little bit of magic,

and a whole lot of nonsense.

Cover and illustrations by Zoe Saunders.

A CIP catalogue record for this book is available from the British Library.

Published in 2023 by Whimsicolour Publishing.

Paperback ISBN: 978-1-9164352-3-0
Hardcover ISBN: 978-1-9164352-4-7

Hetty Honeywort and the Dragon Disaster

By Zoe Saunders

Meet the Characters...

Our Reluctant Heroes...

Hetty Honeywort
(a rubbish witch)

Penelope Yellowlegs
(her talking
chicken familiar*)

* By the way, a 'familiar' is an animal who is both a friend and an assistant to a witch, and helps them with their magical tasks and chores.

For Penelope, this mostly involves making cups of tea and tidying spell bottles.

The Sidekicks...
His Royal Highness
Prince Cuthbert
the Third
(a daft prince)
Derek
(a grumpy
llama)

The Dragon

The villain of this story...

...Or is she?

And these guys...
(You'll meet them later)

Contents

Chapter One

Hetty Honeywort was a terrible witch.

I don't mean terrible as in, '*luring innocent children to a gingerbread cottage in the middle of a dark forest, then roasting them in a whopping great big boiling hot oven*,' sort of terrible.

I mean terrible as in, really, rather rubbish.

For a start, she didn't *look* much like a witch. She wasn't tall, dark, and spindly. She didn't have long black hair, or a wart on her nose, or pointy boots.

She *did* wear a pointy hat, but it wasn't *tall* and pointy, like a proper witch's hat. Hetty's hat was short and stubby, just like her.

She wore round glasses, and had reddish, wavy hair, along with a smattering of freckles over her button nose; hardly 'witch-like' at all!

She was, to her dismay, quite adorable.

Hetty told everyone her dream of becoming a wicked witch had been ruined from the moment they'd given her a chicken as a familiar, back in Witch School. After all, have you ever heard of an all-powerful wicked witch with a chicken as a familiar? Of course you haven't, especially a talking chicken named Penelope Yellowlegs.

The truth was Hetty just didn't have it in her — wickedness that is. She'd rather be pottering about in her garden, or drinking tea, or eating cake, than casting evil spells. It was all far too much excitement, and way too much effort. And Hetty liked a quiet life.

Now, we know Hetty wasn't the best at being a 'wicked' witch, but she wasn't brilliant at being a 'good' witch either. All that prancing around in long, frilly dresses, singing to the animals and rescuing handsome princes in distress? Oh no, that wasn't Hetty's cup of tea at all. The thought of spending all day twirling around in a frilly dress made Hetty's nose wrinkle in disgust. She liked to wear dungarees, not dresses. Not to mention her singing voice sounded more like a strangled cat than a nightingale.

So Hetty Honeywort was neither good, nor bad, but a little bit of both — like we all are, I suppose. And her magic was the same; some of it was a little bit good, and some of it was a little bit bad.

Hetty would sometimes put small curses on people who annoyed her. They were never anything *really* nasty, more like mild annoyances. Such as the time Barnaby Bramblebottom pushed in front of her in the bakery queue. Barnaby had snaffled the last strawberry cream bun even though he had *seen* Hetty looking at it. The cheek!

After Hetty's curse, any time Barnaby tried to dip a biscuit into his mug of tea, it would snap, sink to the bottom of the mug, and turn into biscuity sludge.

The same thing happened again and again, and it would happen forever more. A deserving curse for being so rude, Hetty thought.

Hetty knew enough good magic to heal small ailments, like ingrowing toenails, nose pimples, or the hiccups. This was enough to keep her on good 'non-pitchfork' terms with the local villagers. She ran a monthly pimple clinic, every second Tuesday of the month, and was happy to be paid in cake or biscuits for her healing ointments.

One thing Hetty *longed* to be able to do was make a proper spell potion. But so far, despite years of practice, she'd only been able to cook up hundreds of rather useless ones. Something always went wrong during the process. More often than not, it was an incorrect ingredient, and at other times it was a *missing* ingredient. She also had a nasty habit of mispronouncing magic words. Whatever it was, it always ended up with the potion having a completely different purpose from the one it was supposed to have in the first place. It was usually something very silly.

Nevertheless, she always carefully poured the potions into small bottles and crammed them onto her shelf '*just in case she needed them*'. Each bottle was labelled with Hetty's scratchy handwriting, so that she knew what it was. The descriptions read things like 'Laughter Juice', 'Hairy Feet Lotion', 'Sneezing Syrup', and 'Bushy Beard Growing Elixir (Strawberry Flavoured)'.

You'd think with her life being so mundane, Hetty would be a miserable soul. You'd think that she'd be terribly jealous of all the other, more *witchy*, witches. But this simply wasn't the case.

Hetty was perfectly happy living her quiet life, in her little thatched cottage in the middle of the forest.

Every night, she would happily snuggle down in her bed next to Penelope, pull her patchwork quilt right up under her chin, wriggle her toes contentedly, and reflect on what a perfectly charming life she led. It was peaceful, calm, and beautifully boring, just the way she liked it.

The last thing Hetty Honeywort wanted
was an adventure.

Chapter Two

Springtime had arrived in the forest. Shafts of golden sunlight peeked through the branches of the budding trees, and tiny snowdrops were sprouting beneath the ancient oak. In a nearby clearing was Hetty Honeywort's little house. It had a yellow door, a thatched roof, and a wonky chimney.

Inside, Hetty and her familiar, Penelope the chicken, were making themselves breakfast—a big pot of tea and a generous slice of cake. Hetty had cake for most meals. This morning, it was apple and cinnamon cake.

Hetty sat down in her comfy armchair with her plate on her lap. She placed the teacup and saucer precariously on the arm and was about to take a bite out of her cake, when she heard an almighty commotion outside; screaming and shouting, along with the sounds of pattering footsteps as people ran up and down.

Hetty frowned and put her slice of cake back down on the plate. If there was one thing that annoyed her, it was the sound of people running about and shouting, *especially on a Sunday morning.*

She got up and opened the door to see what all the hullabaloo was about. Outside, there were lots of villagers running all over the place, like a flock of headless chickens in a panic.

"Oh Hetty!" they cried, rushing over and bustling around her. "You must help us! It's the **dragon**, she's gone mad! She's gone bananas! She's gone loopy!! She's gone stark raving bonkers!!!"

Hetty folded her arms and scowled. "The **dragon**? What's wrong with the **dragon**?"

"She's scorched all my sheep!"
cried Fargo the Farmer.

"She's toasted all my trout!"
yelled Felix the Fishmonger.

"She's sizzled all my sausages!"
shouted Bob the Butcher.

"She's frazzled all my flowers!"
screeched Felicity the Florist.

"She's burned all my buns!"
wailed Brenda the Baker.

"And all my chickens have disappeared!"
roared Egbert, the egg farmer.

Hetty nodded and said, "Yes, hmm, that's terrible. And, do tell me... What has all this got to do with me?"

"You're a witch!" they cried. "You've got magical powers. Go to the **dragon's** cave and stop her!"

"Me? Why should I stop her?" said Hetty. "I'm not even a powerful witch. What about Mervin the wizard, who lives in the castle with the king? He'd be much better at fighting **dragons** than me."

"Oh, we already asked him," said one of the villagers. "He says he doesn't do **dragons**."

"Doesn't *do* **dragons**? Whatever do you mean?" said Hetty, feeling annoyed.

"He says he's allergic," the villager replied. "Apparently they bring him out in a terrible rash."

"Pah! A likely excuse!" said Hetty with a snort. "Allergic to **dragons** indeed. Now, if you don't mind, I was just having my breakfast. I think you'll find this is none of my business. I wish you the best of luck with your **dragon** problem. Goodbye!"

Hetty turned around to go back into her house and get back to the important business of eating cake.

However, before she could get through the door, a huge, dark shadow loomed overhead. She looked up to see the disgruntled **dragon** flying above, her shiny green scales glinting in the sunlight. The **dragon** took a deep breath and blew a jet of hot red flames from her nostrils and set the roof of Hetty's house alight. Fire danced on the thatched straw roof, and grey smoke billowed into the air.

"Well, would you look at that..." said Hetty, looking irritated as her thatched roof burned. "It looks like it *is* my business after all."

"See! We told you! She's out of control!" said the villagers, jumping up and down. "You'll have to go and stop her!"

Hetty's eyes followed the **dragon** as she flew away and became smaller and smaller in the distance. She soared high up into the mountains, and disappeared amongst the clouds.

"Oh no. She lives all the way up there?" Hetty said disappointedly. "Crumbling cabbages! It'll take me weeks to walk all the way up there. I've only got short legs!"

"What about your broomstick Missus?" one of the village children shouted. "All witches have a broomstick, don't they?"

"It's gone to the mechanics." Hetty replied. "It's got a faulty sparkle plug. It'll be weeks before I get it back."

"You can take my llama!" A thin man walked forward leading a fluffy white llama, who had a rather grumpy face. "He's very sure-footed. He'll get you up the mountain, no problem at all. His name is Derek."

The man handed the llama's halter rope to Hetty.

Derek looked down his nose at her with a scowl.

"Erm... Does he spit?" asked Hetty, feeling nervous.

"Yep!" said the villager. "Never stops spitting!"

As he walked away, Derek spat in the man's direction. The ball of slime whizzed past the man's ear, missing him by an inch, before hitting a tree and glooping down the bark.

"Alright then," said Hetty, taking a step away from the llama. "And what am I supposed to do when I get up to the **dragon's** cave? I'm hardly the sort to be fighting **dragons**, am I?"

The villagers muttered and whispered amongst themselves. Then Hetty heard gasps of surprise.

The crowd parted, to reveal His Royal Highness, Prince Cuthbert the Third, wearing his shiniest suit of armour. He was carrying a huge sword and a golden shield with his own portrait engraved on the front of it. On his head was a tall helmet with a huge purple feather poking out of the top.

He looked quite ridiculous, Hetty thought.

Prince Cuthbert the Third strode forward with a toothy smile, and took a deep bow.

"At your service, Your Witchiness," he said in his silly, posh voice. "I bid you my sword, my shield, and my immense, unwavering bravery, on your great quest into the mountains."

Some of the women swooned and fanned themselves with their hands. Hetty rolled her eyes. She had a distinct feeling that Prince Cuthbert would be more trouble than he was worth.

"FINE!" Hetty gave in. "I'll go up to the mountains and sort out this **dragon** problem. Then I hope you will all leave me in peace!"

"We will! We will! "chimed the villagers. "Oh thank you Hetty! Thank you, Prince Cuthbert!"

Hetty huffed in annoyance, and then went back inside her house to collect a few things for the journey. She wrapped up plenty of cake in greaseproof paper and put it in her dungaree pockets. She also took a big flask of hot water, some biscuits, teacups, plates, spoons, a tea pot, tea bags, sugar, milk, blankets, a pillow, her toothbrush, a scarf, and something to read. Then she grabbed and armful of potion bottles from her shelf because you *never know when they might come in useful.*

All of it went into her dungaree pockets.

In case you're wondering how on earth she could fit so much into her pockets, I should tell you that Hetty's dungaree pockets were magical . She could hold an almost infinite number of objects inside them.

"Penelope! Penelope! Where are you?" Hetty called out, before whipping back a little pair of curtains which shielded a small, straw-filled wicker basket in the corner of the room. Penelope was sitting in the basket, reading a newspaper.

"Do you MIND?!" said Penelope, almost dropping her newspaper in shock. "I am laying my EGG!"

"Well, hurry up," said Hetty, snapping the curtains shut again. "We are going on an adventure, and we need to leave *right away*."

"An adventure?" came Penelope's muffled reply from behind the curtains. "But it's *Sunday morning*."

"Well, it seems that adventure waits for no witch..." said Hetty wistfully. "And besides, the roof is on fire."

"The roof is WHAT?!" bakawed Penelope, bursting out from behind the curtains (her poor egg cracking on the ground as it popped out).

"Well why didn't you say so? Let's get out of here!"

Chapter Three

When Hetty and Penelope got back outside, Prince Cuthbert the Third was already sitting on top of Derek. Derek didn't look too pleased about the situation.

"Who said you could ride Derek?" said Hetty, folding her arms.

"Well, I thought it was only fair," said the prince. "After all, I AM the prince, and I AM wearing all this heavy silver armour, and I AM the most important person here. Not to mention I need to conserve my energy for fighting that beastly **dragon**."

Hetty was just about to protest further, when an elderly man hobbled forward, and handed her a tatty paper scroll. "You'll need this my dear," he croaked. "It's a map."

Hetty unrolled the paper scroll to reveal an old, hand-drawn map showing the whole kingdom. She could see the king's palace, and the little villages on its outskirts. She could also see her forest, and some other places she'd never heard of before (she didn't get out much). Hetty tilted her head, and turned the map sideways, then upside down, trying to see the best route to the **dragon**'s cave. The old man shuffled up next to her.

"All you need to do..." he said, prodding the map and then tracing a wobbly line across it with his wrinkled finger, "...is walk along here through the Meadow of Misery. Then, you need to find your way through the Fearsome Fairy Forest. Most people get lost forever in there, but if *you* don't, you'll find yourselves at the Blue Lagoon of Doom. Use the Slimy Stepping stones of Death to make your way across. And if you're still alive after all that, you can start climbing the Misty Mountain to find the **dragon**'s cave."

"Meadow of Misery? Fearsome Fairy Forest? Blue Lagoon of Doom?!" said Hetty, with a nervous gulp.

"Piece of cake!" exclaimed Prince Cuthbert the Third. "A simple task for a fearless, battle-trained, talented and handsome prince — such as myself."

Hetty thought with any luck she'd be able to lose Prince Cuthbert the Third in the Meadow of Misery. Or perhaps she could give him away to the fairies in the fearsome forest, if they'd have him that is.

"And I see you've bought us some supper for later," Prince Cuthbert grinned, pointing at Penelope. "What a marvellous idea! I DO love roast chicken!"

"How dare you!" said Penelope, ruffling her feathers. "I am not SUPPER. I'll have you know I am a very **rare** and **important** magical chicken *familiar*. Thank you very much!"

"Well, I never," said Prince Cuthbert. "Amazing! A talking chicken! Ho ho! Whatever next? Hey. Here's a good one... Why did the chicken cross the road?"

"To **peck** the stupid prince right on the end of his big pompous nose," replied Penelope crossly, folding her wings.

"Well, that's a bit rude," said the prince, looking deflated. "It was only a joke."

"Enough!" shouted Hetty. "We need to get going. We've got a long journey ahead of us."

Hetty lifted Penelope up and let her perch on her shoulder, then strode away at a brisk pace. Prince Cuthbert flapped Derek's reins and said, "YA!" to make him walk. Derek grunted and then spat in irritation. The goblet of spit hit an old woman right in the face.

"Ergghh!" she shrieked.

The villagers formed a crowd as Hetty, Penelope, Prince Cuthbert and Derek walked by. They all cheered and sobbed and waved their handkerchiefs as they said farewell.

"Good luck!" they cried. "Hope you all don't die!"

"Goodbye my faithful peasants!" said Prince Cuthbert, as he waved back at the crowd from high up on Derek's back. "Have no fear! Prince Cuthbert the Third will save you all from the fearsome fire-breathing **dragon**! *I'm very brave you know.*"

A young woman squealed and threw a red rose as he passed her. "Love you Prince Cuthbert!" she yelled.

The prince caught the rose as it sailed through the air. He sniffed it delicately, before winking at the young woman, who promptly fainted.

"I do NOT see the appeal," Penelope whispered into Hetty's ear. "He's very annoying."

"He is also very rich," Hetty whispered back. "And on the lookout for a girl to marry and make into a Princess."

Leaving the cheering villagers behind, they walked

through the forest until they came to the edge. Hetty's tummy fluttered with nerves as she stepped out from under the trees into the bright daylight. She usually didn't stray far from the forest, and she felt homesick already.

According to the map, the Meadow of Misery was over the next hill. Hetty's legs were already aching, and Penelope was heavy on her shoulder. But the little chicken had dozed off to sleep and Hetty hadn't the heart to tell her to get off and walk.

As he rode along on Derek, Prince Cuthbert the Third prattled on and on, about himself mostly.

"Mummy said it was about time I went on an adventure," he said. "She said no girl will want to marry a prince who hasn't killed a **dragon** before. Well, it doesn't have to be a **dragon**. I suppose an ogre or a giant or a sea serpent would do just as well. But a **dragon** is what will *really* impress the girls. And Daddy told me I was a wet lettuce who needs to be toughened up. Haha! He *does* like to make jokes, but he doesn't mean it... At least I don't think he does."

Hetty wasn't really listening. She was thinking about the cake and biscuits in her dungaree pockets, and wondering how soon would be considered *too soon* to have a quick tea break.

"My cousin Tarquin, now *he* married a very pretty girl after he beheaded a ghastly giant which was roaming around stomping on villagers and squishing them like bugs. He was practically fighting the girls off after that. And my half-cousin once-removed, Fabio, he got married to a lovely blonde-haired beauty, after he killed a Sabre-toothed Snufflewuffle, which is sort of like a gigantic hamster... He *did* lose an arm though, pity..."

"I think we're here!" said Penelope, who had just woken up from her nap. "Look!"

There in the near distance was the Meadow of Misery; a vast rippling sea of swaying grass, with some small flowers growing here and there.

"Well, it doesn't look so miserable to me," said Prince Cuthbert. "I don't know what all the fuss is about. Come on Derek, my faithful steed. I bet you're hungry. You can eat some of that grass. Best keep your strength up, old boy!"

Derek licked his lips, bellowed, and began to march forward with determination.

"Wait a second. Stop!" shouted Hetty. "What's that noise?"

"What noise?" said Prince Cuthbert. "I don't hear any noise. Nothing at—"

"Well, if you'd stop yapping for one second," said Penelope.

They were all quiet and still, and then they heard it. It was a sort of wailing, crying noise.

"Waaaaahhhhhhhhhhuhhhhhh!
Sniff-Sniff...
Waaaaaaaaaaaaaaaaahhuuuhuhhhh!"

The ghastly sound was full of sorrow and torment. It made the skin on Hetty's arms go all goosebumpy.

"Waaaaaahhhuhhhhhhhhhhhh!"

"What in the sizzling sausages is that noise?"
Hetty whispered.
"It almost sounds like a... like a... g-g-ghost."

Chapter Four

Most witches don't mind ghosts at all, but as we have already learned, Hetty was not like most witches. And apart from a few friendly ghosts and ghouls who she knew personally, she found them very frightening.

"It d-d-does sound like a g-g-ghost," said Prince Cuthbert the Third, who had turned as pale as a ghost himself.

Even Derek's eyes were bulging with fear. He let out a nervous spit.

"It sounds like a ghost with a runny nose," said Penelope haughtily. "Why does it keep sniffling? Ghosts don't sniffle!"

Penelope, despite being a chicken (a creature with a reputation for being cowardly) was the bravest of the lot of them. She hopped off Hetty's shoulder and began to march towards the meadow.

Hetty and Prince Cuthbert looked at each other, shrugged their shoulders, and then followed the brave little chicken towards the meadow... And the spooky wailing noise.

As they stepped into the long grass and trudged forward, the noise stopped, and an eerie hush fell. The only sound was the rustling of grass in the gentle breeze. It was quiet.

Almost too quiet.

"Oh look, how splendid!" said Prince Cuthbert, as he noticed something on the ground. "Mummy has flowers like that in her greenhouse back at the castle. She loves collecting rare species. They're *just* like this one, only much bigger."

He jumped down from Derek's back to inspect a little purplish-blue flower. He reached down and plucked it out of the ground.

The prince held the little flower up to his nose and took a sniff. "Ahhh, that sweet aroma! Reminds me of home," he said.

Suddenly, tiny, high-pitched battle cries rang out all around them. They were leaped upon by hundreds of tiny, turnip shaped creatures with round bodies and flowers growing out of the top of their heads. The creatures were small, but they had a very nasty nip!

Prince Cuthbert the Third drew his sword, and spun around on the spot bellowing,

"BE GONE FOUL IMPS!"

Hetty held on to her hat, and ran as fast as her legs could carry her. Penelope sprinted around in circles, squawking and flapping her wings. Derek kicked and spit as one attached itself to his leg and sunk it's tiny teeth in.

Still the little creatures kept coming. They pulled off Hetty's Hat, tossed it into the floor, and then grabbed onto her hair, yanking it viciously. Then they tied her bootlaces together, making her tumble over onto the ground.

"Waaaaaahhhhh!" she cried, as she landed with a bump.

"They're pulling out my tail feathers!" clucked Penelope. "My beautiful tail feathers! Oh, stop it! You little rotters!"

Derek tried to aim spitballs at his tiny attackers, but he kept missing and hitting Prince Cuthbert instead. The spitballs made a 'Puh-TING!' sound, as they hit his metal armor.

One large goblet of spit hit the visor of Prince Cuthbert's helmet, making it drop down over his face, leaving him with only a thin slit to see out of.

"I CAN'T SEE!" he wailed, still spinning around holding his sword. "I'm getting DIZZY!"

Prince Cuthbert tripped over Hetty, who was still on the floor with her bootlaces tied together. Derek tripped over Prince Cuthbert, squashing him flat, and Penelope ran around them in a circle, feathers flying everywhere.

"Haven't you packed some of your silly spells?" said Penelope, breathless as she ran around and around, followed by a pack of angry little turnip people. "Surely there's *something* you can use to make them stop?!"

"Good idea Penelope!" said Hetty. She rummaged through her dungaree pockets, pulling out lots of small spell bottles and reading the labels. "Purple Beard Growing Syrup... No that's no use... What about... Double-in-Size Potion? Oh gibbering giblets not that one, that's the *last* thing we need. Erm... how about this one? Hiccuping Juice?"

"Just DO something! And HURRY!" shouted Penelope, who was exhausted from all the running.

Hetty popped the cork off the little bottle of 'Hiccuping Juice'. She held the bottle above her head, and waved her arm about, scattering little droplets of the potion all around her.

The little turnip creatures slowed down. Then they stood still. And then they started to produce tiny, high-pitched little hiccups.

"Hiccup!

Hiccup!

Hiccup!"

Penelope, Prince Cuthbert, and Derek also started to hiccup.

"HICCUP! Oh my... HICCUP! I *do* beg your pardon... HICCUP!" said the prince.

"HIC-CLUCK! HIC-CLUCK!... Hetty what on earth have you HIC-CLUCK! done?!" said Penelope.

"I was trying to HELP!" said Hetty. "They stopped biting you, didn't they? That means my spell worked."

Hetty didn't have the hiccups because, just by chance, none of the potion droplets had landed on her. She untied her knotted bootlaces, put her hat back on, and crawled over to one of the tiny, hiccupping turnip creatures to get a closer look.

"Hiccup!" it said, before falling backwards onto its bottom. The creature's little face looked sad and worried.

"Oh, it's really rather cute," said Hetty, as she peered down at it. "Come on little one. Let me sort out those nasty hiccups for you."

Hetty held out her hand and the little creature jumped onto it. Using one finger, Hetty rubbed and patted its back, like she was burping a baby. "There, there," she said soothingly.

The little creature let out a few more hiccups, and then a little burp.

"There. That's better isn't it? Those naughty hiccups have all gone. Now, why don't you tell me what this is about?" said Hetty. "Who are you? And why are you attacking us?"

"We are the Sproutlings," came a squeaky voice from the little creature. "We're only babies. Someone took our mummies away, and we miss them very much. That's why we cry all the time."

"Oh dear," said Hetty, putting the first sproutling down, then picking up another and patting it on the back with her finger gently to ease its hiccups. "Someone stole your mothers. How very upsetting."

"And then, when that big shiny one Hiccup! came and pulled one of us out of the ground Hiccup! we all got very cross! We don't like being PICKED!" The tiny sproutling pointed at Prince Cuthbert.

"Oh my, HICCUP!" he said. "I am *most* HICCUP! Sorry about that. I didn't HICCUP! realize you little fellows were alive."

"All plants and flowers are alive — you big nincompoop!" said one of the sproutlings.

"So, this is all your HIC-CLUCK! fault," said Penelope, glaring accusingly at Prince Cuthbert.

"Prince Cuthbert?" said Hetty. "Didn't you say your mother had some flowers like these? In her greenhouse?"

"Oh yes, HICCUP! She does," replied Prince Cuthbert. "*Remarkably* similar. They even smell the same."

"Where did she get them?" said Hetty.

"Mervin the wizard magicked them up for her," said Prince Cuthbert smugly.

"Hmm," Hetty nodded, and then she leaned down to the little sproutlings, who had gathered around her, all waiting to be patted on the back.

"I think I know where your mummies might be," she said.

Chapter Five

After everyone had finally stopped hiccupping, Hetty laid down a blanket on the grass so that they could all sit down for a rest and maybe a little nap.

"Let's have some tea and biscuits," she said.

Hetty removed the flask, teapot, tea, milk, sugar and cups from her dungaree pockets, along with a tin of raspberry and white chocolate chip cookies. She offered one to the sproutlings.

"Oh no, we don't like biscuits," they said. "Yuk!"

"Oh," said Hetty, feeling bemused. She'd never met anyone who didn't like biscuits before, especially raspberry and white chocolate chip cookies. "Well, what *do* you like to eat?" asked Hetty curiously.

"**WORM POO**," they said with a grin. "It's yummy scrummy!

"Worm poo?" said Hetty, feeling a bit sick. "But I don't have any—"

"I'll find some worms!" said Penelope, jumping up to her feet. Penelope was partial to an occasional plate of worms for supper, after all, she was a chicken. "I'll squeeze all the poo out of them for you," she said cheerfully. "Then I will enjoy the worms."

"Ewhh," Prince Cuthbert pulled a face. "Worm poop, how very uncouth."

A sip of tea instantly made Hetty feel much better. She sighed deeply, then nibbled on a cookie. "I promise we will return your mothers just as soon as we get back from sorting out this fire-breathing nuisance of a **dragon**," she said to the sproutlings.

The sproutlings sat munching on their **WORM POO**, which Penelope had just squeezed out of the worms like toothpaste out of a tube.

"*If* we get back," said Penelope, slurping up a long wriggling worm and then gulping it down. "First we've got to find our way through the Fearsome Fairy Forest, then we need to cross the Blue Lagoon of Doom, and then climb up the Misty Mountain to the **dragon**... And *then* we've got to get back again... Alive!"

"You're going through the Fairy Forest?" squeaked a little sproutling. "Oh dear me..."

"Yes, that's where we are going next," replied Hetty. "Why?"

"Oohh, it's very dangerous in there. Once you go in, you never come out. People get lost forever in that forest," said the sproutling. "And those fairies are real meanies!"

"I'm sure we will be fine," said Hetty, who was really *not* sure that they would be fine. "We will get going first thing in the morning. The sooner we sort out this **dragon**, the sooner we can get back home."

"SNIFF, SNIFF, SNIFFFLE..."

Everyone turned to look at Prince Cuthbert, whose lower lip was poking out and trembling.

"Whatever's the matter?" said Penelope.

The prince replied, "I was just thinking about these poor little sproglings—"

"Sproutlings!" they corrected him.

"—and how they missed their poor mothers, and then I realized that... I realized... that... that... I miss my MUMMY too!"

He took a deep breath and burst into tears.

"WAAAAAAAAAAAAAHHHHH!"

"Erm. There, there," said Hetty, moving over to sit beside the prince, and awkwardly patting him on the back. "We're all a little homesick, aren't we everyone?"

Hetty patted the prince on the back, offered him some more tea, and said, "*There, there,*" lots more times. But try as she might, she could not console the prince enough to get him to stop crying. Now that he had started, it seemed he couldn't stop. He bawled, and wailed, and sniffled, and cried out for his...

"MUUUMMMMYYYYYY!"

The poor little sproutlings covered their ears and squeaked, "Make him stop. *Please!*"

"Yes, make him stop for goodness' sake!" said Penelope, who had plucked some feathers from the underside of her tummy and stuffed them into her ear holes. "He's giving me a spiffling headache!"

Derek bellowed forlornly, and then spat.

"Alright, calm down everyone," said Hetty. "I probably have a spell for this somewhere..."

She emptied her dungaree pockets of spell bottles, gathered them all together on the floor, and searched through them for a potion that might stop the prince's wailing.

"Hairy Feet Lotion... Giant Bubble Blowing Potion.... Jumping Juice... Singing Syrup..."

"Try that one!" said Penelope. "Even singing has to be better than this!"

"Ok, Singing Syrup it is," said Hetty. "Here we go."

Hetty took the shiny little bottle, pulled out the cork with a pop, and tipped the pink liquid into the open, wailing mouth of Prince Cuthbert.

Prince Cuthbert gulped. Then he coughed and spluttered. Then he let out a huge Buurrrrp!

And then, he placed a hand on his puffed-out chest, took a deep breath, and started singing a warbling tune at a very high, falsetto pitch.

"Ohhhhhhh,
The mighty Prince went on a quest,
As brave as brave could be.
He went to slay a dragon,
Without his sweet Mummy.

Riding Derek, his faithful steed,
The brave prince came to meadow.
He stopped to pick a pretty flower,
Which turned out to be a little angry fellow."

"Make him stop!" the sproutlings squeaked. "Make him stop! Make him stop!"

"I *did* make him stop," said Hetty. "I made him stop crying — isn't that what you wanted?"

"Yes. But we don't like this either," they said. "In fact, we prefer the crying."

"The Sproglings attacked the handsome prince,
And he fought them with all his might.
Brave of heart, he swung his sword,
And gave the little imps a fright."

"That's not even how it happened," the sproutlings complained. "He didn't frighten us at all. He's singing fibs."

"I didn't think it was possible," said Penelope with a frown, "but you seem to have made him even *more* annoying."

"Well, I'm sorry but can't do anything about it now," said Hetty. "We'll just have to wait for the spell to wear off."

"How long will that take?" said Penelope.

"I don't know," said Hetty. "It could be days..."

"Days?!" the sproutlings chimed.

"DAYS?!" squawked Penelope.

Derek spat.

"I think it's time for you to leave now," said the sproutlings.

"But it'll be night time soon," said Penelope. "Can't we just stay until the morning?"

"Nope," the sproutlings replied. "Not with *him* making that racket."

"The prince stopped for a little rest,
Some biccies and a spot of tea.
But before he could have a nappy nap,
The Sproglings demanded he leave."

"Fair enough," sighed Hetty. "Come on Your Highness, get back up on Derek. We have to go."

The singing prince mounted the llama, his armor clanging as he climbed aboard. Derek bellowed his disapproval at having him so near to his ear holes.

Llamas have very sensitive ears you see, and they really REALLY despise singing. They hate whistling the most, but singing comes a close second.

"Here you go Derek," said Hetty, popping the two corks she had left from the empty spell bottles into his ears to block out the noise.

Derek seemed a little happier now that he couldn't hear the prince. Well, maybe not happy, but certainly a little less grumpy.

"Ohhhhhhhh,
Derek is a magnificent beast,
Upon his back the brave prince sits.
A faithful steed, he leads the way,
But be careful because he spits."

Chapter Six

The Fearsome Fairy Forest loomed before them, shrouded in mist. The gnarled trees creaked and swayed, their leaves gently rustling in the breeze.

All around, there were wonky, hand-painted signs hanging off the branches, saying, "**KEEP OUT**" and "**NO BIG PEOPLE**" and, "**FAIRIES ONLY**".

"Oh," said Penelope as she studied the signs. "It looks like we can't go in here. We're not allowed."

"But we've GOT to go through the forest," said Hetty. "It's on the map."

Prince Cuthbert pulled Derek to a halt, cleared his throat, and then warbled,

"The fairy forest blocks our path,
To the Blue Lagoon of Doom.
There is no other way around,
So, let's go onward into the gloom."

"He's right, you know," said Hetty to Penelope. "We've got to go through the forest, no matter what the signs say."

So, they all took a deep breath, and stepped into the shadows of the trees. The ground underfoot was soft and mossy, and despite the gloom, bluebells flowered all around. They carefully trod their way through, being cautious to not step on any of the delicate blooms.

They crossed a small, sparkling stream where little silvery fish swam in the shallows.

Over the other side of the stream, the group came upon a huge oak tree, with branches that were so long and heavy that they curved over and bent right back down to the forest floor. They stepped over the gnarled roots and ducked under the low hanging boughs.

Beyond the ancient oak tree, they came to a thick, wooded area, where the tall trees grew so close together that they blocked out what little daylight there was left. It was so dark they could hardly see.

"I'm a bit scared," said Penelope. "Pick me up Hetty, chickens don't like the dark."

Hetty lifted Penelope and held her soft body in her arms. The group kept walking, wide-eyed and silent through the murkiness. Slowly, the trees thinned, and the dusky light made its way back down to the forest floor, until they could just about see again.

A clearing opened out in front of them, with a carpet of soft moss underfoot and swathes of pretty bluebells. They trod carefully through the sweet-smelling flowers, until they came upon a trickling stream where small silvery fishes swam in the shallows. Crossing the little stream with a hop, they found a magnificent oak tree. It's branches were so long and heavy that they curved over and bent right back down to the forest floor. They stepped over the gnarled roots and ducked under the low hanging bows.

"*Hang on a minute*," said Penelope. "We've been here before, I'm sure of it." She looked around curiously. "I remember this tree."

Hetty gasped. "Oh Fizzlepips! You're right Penelope. We *have* been here before. We've been walking around in a whopping big circle!"

"The forest leads us on a merry dance,
Around and around and around.
Let us take a right turn here,
And maybe a path can be found."

sang the prince, pointing in the direction he thought they should go.

"I wish he'd shut up singing," said Penelope. "He's driving me potty."

"But I do think he's right," said Hetty. "Let's stop going straight, or what we've been *thinking* is straight. Instead, let's take slight right turn here."

Prince Cuthbert and Derek led the way, this time turning slightly to the right.

Derek's hoofbeats echoed amongst the trees, making a background beat to the prince's tune.

"The handsome prince bravely leads the way,
Without a shred of fear,
And soon we will reach the Lagoon of Doom,
I can feel it is very neaAAAAARRRGGHHHH!

Penelope and Hetty watched in horror as the ground before them seemed to open up and swallow Prince Cuthbert and Derek whole. Prince Cuthbert screamed, Derek bellowed, and then there was a loud THUD! And then another even louder THUD!

"Yipes!" cried Hetty, dropping Penelope and dashing over as fast as she could.

Prince Cuthbert and Derek had fallen into a trap. It was a deep pit with steep, slippery sides, and absolutely no way to climb out. They were well and truly stuck. Penelope and Hetty peered over the edge into the darkness.

"Are you alright down there?" said Penelope. "Are you hurt?"

From down the dark hole, there came a shaky tune,

"Derek and the handsome Prince,
Have fallen into a pit.
Luckily, we have no injuries,
We're shaken, but perfectly fit."

"Well, at least you're alright." said Hetty.

"But how on earth will we get them out?" clucked Penelope. Then, a wry smile came over her beak. "Or... *Here's an idea...* Shall we just *leave him*? He *is* very annoying after all."

"No Penelope, I don't think we should leave him," Hetty said, though admittedly she was tempted."Besides, poor Derek's down there too."

"Aha!" came a shrill voice from behind them. "We have caught you! Didn't you read the signs? We said NO BIG PEOPLE! And you didn't listen, and now we have captured you!"

"Who said that?" said Hetty, her eyes searching the gloom for the owner of the voice. She couldn't see anyone. "Show yourself!"

"Up here!" said the voice, coming from above.

Hetty looked up to see a brightly glowing fairy hovering above her head. The fairy was very, very small. So small that you could have mistaken her for a tiny firefly. She had a sharp little face, pointed ears, and her wings sparkled like jewels.

She was soon joined by a more fairies, and they fluttered around in the air. The fairies whispered to each other, occasionally looking over their shoulders at Hetty.

From deep down in the pit, Prince Cuthbert could see the glowing fairies too.

"Oh, what lovely little sparkles,
Shining in the gloom.
They remind me of the fairy lights,
Which hang around my room."

"Be quiet, Turnip Brain!" clucked Penelope.

After they'd finished their whispering, the fairies flew down, and fluttered in front of Hetty's face.

"We have decided to take the big shiny one as our hostage," the spokesfairy said, pointing in the direction of the pit. "We are keeping him all until our stolen friends are returned."

"Stolen friends?" said Hetty. "What do you mean? Who stole them?"

"Hundreds of us have been TAKEN!" the fairies cried.

"But who?" said Hetty. "And why?"

"It was that miserable wizard!" said another fairy. "He's got a pointy hat like yours, only his is taller and has stars on it."

"And he's got a white beard!" shouted another.

"He captured our friends in a net, and then he

trapped them inside these little glass balls..." said another.

The Prince's song rose up again out of the deep pit.

"I miss my lovely bedroom,
With my shiny fairy lights.
Mummy says they keep the trolls away,
So I can sleep soundly at night."

"For the last time, shut your cake hole." said Penelope, peering into the pit. "Nobody wants to hear about your silly bedroom and your—"

"*Fairy lights!*" said Hetty, her eyes widening. She stepped over to the edge of the pit and shouted down, "Where did you get your fairy lights Prince Cuthbert?"

Prince Cuthbert replied, in song of course,

"Mervin the wizard gave me a gift,
To help me sleep at night.
A long string of tiny glass balls,
All filled with glowing light."

"Oh no. *He's* got them," said Penelope. "Those poor fairies have been stolen and trapped inside fairy lights. Mervin took the fairies just like he took those flowers."

"I think you're right," replied Hetty. "That wizard has got a lot to answer for." She turned to the fairies. "We think we might know where your friends are. If you let us go, we promise to return them."

The fairies all gathered together and whispered furiously. Then they turned around and said, "We have conferred, and decided that we will keep the shiny one hostage. We heard you call him 'Prince', that means he's very important, and important people make good hostages."

Prince Cuthbert overheard, and floating up from the bottom of the pit came yet another song,

"Oh, please don't keep me captive,
I don't like it down in this pit.
It's dark and I'm claustrophobic,
And covered in Derek's spit."

The fairies looked towards the hole and frowned. Then more whispering, until the spokesfairy turned to Hetty again and said, "But... Just *one* thing before we make our final decision... Erm.. Does he sing like that ALL the time?"

"Yes. I'm afraid so," said Hetty. "He's got a magic spell on him, and I don't know when it will wear off... Or if it will ever wear off at all."

"Oh Shiny fairies please let me go free,
And please release poor Derek too.
Please be quick, I need the toilet,
I'm rather desperate for a P –"

"Enough!" the fairies shouted. "Enough!! OK! We will let you go! Just please STOP SINGING!"

Chapter Seven

With a long rope and a little bit of magic, Hetty, Penelope and the fairies managed to haul Prince Cuthbert and Derek out of the pit. The fairies showed them the way out of the forest (as fast as they possible could, due to Prince Cuthbert's singing). And they were soon ready to continue their journey.

"Goodbye!" said the fairies, waving cheerily. "Don't forget to bring our friends home! Or you'll be sorry!"

"We won't forget," replied Hetty, feeling distressed that her '*to do*' list was getting longer and longer. Now, she didn't just have to fix the **dragon disaster**, but she also needed to rescue the sproutling's mothers, along with the stolen fairies.

"Oh, and be sure to watch out for the Gigantic Dagger-Toothed, Razor-Finned, Lumpy Bumpy Monster Eel which lives in the lake!" the fairies said. "Don't fall in whatever you do!"

"The Gigantic... What?!" said Hetty.

"Never mind! Goodbye!" the fairies replied, disappearing back into the forest.

The Blue Lagoon of Doom was a short trek away from the Fearsome Fairy Forest. It was a huge, wide, deep lake, that would have taken days to walk around. The only way across was a long series of small, slimy stepping stones. The water was dark, glassy, and perfectly still, reflecting the sunset sky as if it were a mirror. Hetty felt herself shiver with fear. Who knew what lurked under the surface.

Hetty inspected the first stepping stone, and tested it with one foot, whilst keeping the other foot on the shore.

The top of the stepping stone was green and slippery, and the sole of her boot slid around on the surface.

"Step aside Witchypoo! I'll go first!" said Prince Cuthbert. "Derek can manage this easily! Llamas are very sure footed you know... *Ohhh*," he sounded disappointed. "I've stopped singing, what a terrible shame. I *do* have such a lovely singing voice. Mummy always says so. Maybe I should carry on singing regardless?"

"NO!" shouted Penelope and Hetty, at the same time.

"Goodness! No need to shout," the prince said. "Yes, I suppose you're right though. Too much of a good thing ruins it. What, what?"

"Erm yes, that's exactly what it is." said Hetty. "Now, let's concentrate on getting across this lake." She frowned. "These stepping stones are as slippery as frog's back covered in pigs grease. We are going to have to be *very carefu—*"

Hetty had hardly finished her sentence, when Prince

Cuthbert cried, "TALLY HO!" and encouraged Derek onward by flapping the reins with great enthusiasm.

Derek bellowed, spat, and then leaped six foot into the air, before landing neatly on the first stone. He then did it again, taking a great leap into the air, before landing neatly with all four feet on the tiny stepping stone.

"Wow. Llamas really are sure footed," said Hetty in amazement, as she watched him go.

Derek and Prince Cuthbert leaped and skipped across the stones with ease. Or at least, Derek skipped across the stones with ease. Prince Cuthbert clung on with all his might, like a big clanging sack of potatoes, as the nimble llama leaped and jumped from stone to stone.

"Come on Penelope," said Hetty. "It's our turn, and I think it's best if you go in my pocket. You'll be safe in there."

"Oh no, not in your pocket," clucked Penelope. "It's a dreadful mess in there, all full of spell bottles and biscuits and cups..."

"It's for the best Penelope. What if you fall in? You know how much you hate getting your feathers wet," Hetty reminded her.

"Very well," said Penelope, allowing Hetty to pick her up. "I do hate it when my feathers get wet. But I am having a good tidy up while I'm in there."

"You do that then," said Hetty, pulling open the pocket on her front, and stuffing Penelope into it head first. Penelope let out a muffled squawk, before disappearing into the magic pocket.

Hetty took a deep breath to steady her nerves, and hopped onto the first stone as gracefully as she could manage. Her feet slid around a little, and she wobbled, and then found her balance.

She let out a sigh of relief, before she hopped onto the next stepping stone. And the next. And the next.

"This isn't as bad..." she said, hopping onto the next stone, "...as I thought."

"THAT'S THE TICKET!" came Prince Cuthbert's voice, from the opposite shore of the lake. He and

Derek had already reached the other side. "YOU'RE DOING MARVELLOUSLY! BRAVO HETTY! WHOOP!"

Hetty looked up at him as he waved and cheered. Being a polite sort, she felt obliged to wave back. But as she did so, she lost her balance.

"Wahh! Woah!" she cried, flapping her arms furiously in an attempt to regain her balance. But it was no good.

SPLA-DOOSH!!

Hetty fell in.

The icy cold water enveloped her, taking her breath away. She sank down, down, down, into the murky waters. Hetty kicked her legs and began swimming up to the surface.

Then, of a sudden, a cavernous, gaping mouth, filled with lots and lots and LOTS of sharp teeth gulped her up, and swallowed her whole.

"Oh FIDDLESTIIIIIIIIICKS!" she cried, as she slid down the monster's slippery gullet and into its stomach. Hetty landed on her bottom in a warm, rather smelly puddle with a splash. The monster's stomach was empty apart from a rusty boat anchor and a pile of old boots, and Hetty of course.

"What the jumping crickets is going on?" said Penelope, her head popping up from Hetty's front pocket. She had a teacup stuck on her head. "Where are we? Why is it so dark? What's that foul smell?"

"Erm... Stay calm Penelope, but we appear to have been eaten by a monster," said Hetty, knowing this would not please Penelope at all.

"Oh *typical*!" clucked Penelope. "I might have known we'd get eaten by a monster eventually!"

"Stop flapping and focus," said Hetty. "Didn't you find any useful spells when you were tidying up in there?"

"What useful spells? You don't make useful spells Hetty," replied Penelope. "You always make a mistake and they come out all wrong and silly. Whoever needs a *Purple Beard Growing Potion*? Or a *Hairy Feet Spell*?"

"Hey! I do SO make useful spells," said Hetty, feeling a little hurt. "Well, sometimes they don't always seem like they're going to be useful. But then they *do* come in useful, in very specific circumstances."

Penelope sighed. "Let me have another look." Her head disappeared again as she went back down into the magical pocket.

A moment later, her head popped out. "I've found something," she said. "Pull me out."

Hetty grabbed onto her and yanked her out of the pocket. "What did you find?"

"I found that ridiculous 'Giant Bubble Blowing Potion'... Can monsters blow bubbles?"

"Well, there's only one way to find out!" said Hetty, grabbing the bottle, pulling out the cork, and tipping the contents out into the monster's stomach.

The surrounding walls of the monster's stomach seemed to quiver, and jerk. The monster let out a huge roar which echoed all around.

"Hold on tight Penelope!" said Hetty, wrapping her arms tight around her chicken familiar.

The monster's stomach jerked, and lurched, and rumbled. And then Hetty and Penelope were ejected at breakneck speed out of the monster's tummy and back into its mouth, as it did a gigantic belch.

The monster huffed, puffed, opened its jaws wide, and then it blew the most gigantic bubble you have ever seen, with Hetty and Penelope stuck inside it. The bubble popped free of the monster's mouth, and hung in the water, right in front of its face.

It glared at them through its enormous, googly eyes, with what looked like a shocked expression. I suppose you would be shocked if you just unexpectedly blew a giant bubble with no warning at all.

The monster had a huge mouth with several rows of pointed white teeth, and a long, slippery body, with sharp, spikey fins running all the way down it's back. It's skin was all lumpy and bumpy, like a toad.

"You must be the Gigantic Dagger-Toothed, Razor-Finned, Lumpy Bumpy Monster Eel," said Hetty, her voice echoing around inside the giant bubble.

The monster blinked a few times, surprised that it was being spoken to. Then it replied, in a deep, bubbly voice,

"That's right. I AM the Gigantic,
Dagger-Toothed, Razor-Finned,
Lumpy Bumpy Monster Eel...

...But you can call me Percy if you like."

Chapter Eight

"Now, listen up, Percy," said Hetty, putting her hands on her hips sternly. "You can't go about swallowing up witches and chickens willy-nilly. It's very rude!"

Hetty's voice echoed around inside the huge bubble, as it bobbed about in front of the monster's face.

Percy blinked a few times. "But it's just that I am SO HUNGRY," he said sadly. "This lake used to be full of beautiful, fat, delicious rainbow fish. But now it's practically empty, apart from me. All I've got to eat is rusty anchors and smelly old boots. I hate eating old boots, the laces get stuck in my teeth."

"What happened to all the fish?" asked Penelope. "Where did they go?"

"I don't know," blubbed Percy. "A big boat with a golden crown painted on the side came one day. It dropped a huge net, scooped up all my beautiful rainbow fish, and then it took them away. I've been starving ever since."

"A golden crown on the side of the boat?" said Hetty. "That sounds like it must have been the king's boat."

"But what would the king want with all those fish?" said Penelope.

We can ask Prince Cuthbert, he'll know," said Hetty, before turning back to speak to Percy. "I am going to try my best to find out where all your fish went. So, would you mind not eating us — just for the time being?"

"Alright," sighed Percy. "But I am still really hungry."

The huge bubble slowly made its way to the surface of the lake. When it got there, it emerged above the water with a 'blip', and then bobbed lazily towards the shore. Upon reaching the shore, it popped, leaving Hetty and Penelope on dry land.

"What a marvellous feat of witchcraft! Bravo!" said Prince Cuthbert, clapping enthusiastically. "A giant bubble! How absolutely inspired!"

"Thanks," said Hetty, grinning. "*See*, Penelope. My potions *are* useful."

Penelope tutted and rolled her eyes, before turning to Prince Cuthbert and sternly saying, "Anyway, we need to ask you something, young man. Does your father, the king, have any sort of affinity for rainbow fish?"

"Oh yes, he most certainly does!" said the prince, with a smile. "You see, Daddy simply LOVES caviar. That's *fish eggs* to you peasants. He eats caviar for breakfast, lunch, and supper every single day. And the caviar of the rainbow fish is the juiciest, sweetest. most delicious caviar ever. So, Mervin made Daddy a great big tank in the banquet hall. Then he filled it with all the rainbow fish he could find. Now Daddy has a constant supply of delicious caviar. Isn't that lovely?"

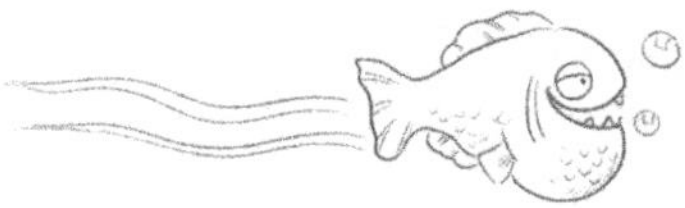

"It's not very lovely for Percy – he's got nothing to eat!" said Penelope.

"Who the devil is Percy?" said the Prince.

"Percy is the Gigantic Dagger-Toothed, Razor-Finned, Lumpy Bumpy Monster Eel, and he lives in this lake," said Hetty. "He just ate us both. But then he kindly coughed us both up inside this bubble, and allowed us to go free."

"And we have promised him he can have his fish back," said Penelope.

"Oh, I'm not sure Daddy will be happy to do that," said Prince Cuthbert. "He really loves his caviar."

"Well, I will have to think of a way to make him," said Hetty, as her stomach rumbled loudly. "Anyway, is it time for tea?"

"Oh yes, yes!" said Prince Cuthbert and Penelope together. "Tea and cake! Tea and cake!"

Hetty pulled a blanket from her dungaree pockets

and laid it down on the grass. Then she took out her teapot, cups, tea, milk, sugar and a few slices of sticky ginger cake. As they ate, Derek nibbled at the grass contentedly. It wasn't long before Hetty started to feel very tired. Full of warm tea and ginger cake, she decided she would rest her eyes, for just a minute. And she fell soundly asleep for the night.

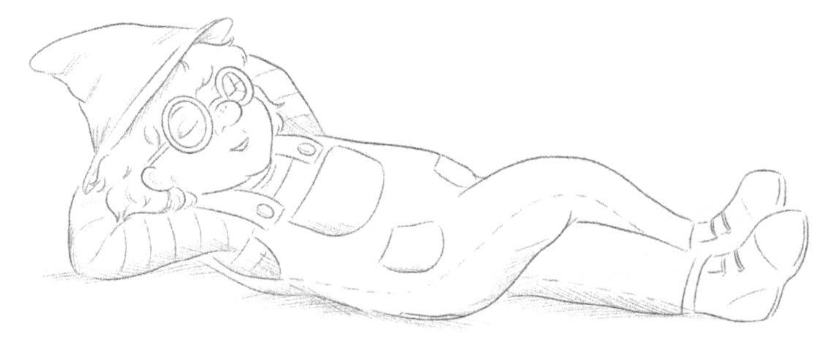

"Hetty! Hetty!" Penelope's clucking woke her up early the next morning.

"What? What?" said Hetty, sitting up and rubbing her sleepy eyes.

"It's the Prince, he's wandering off. Look, there he goes." Penelope pointed over in the distance at the prince, who seemed to be following something through the long grass. He kept looking around, then, dashing forwards, then pouncing.

Hetty reluctantly got up, dusted herself down and tidied up, putting all her things back into her dungaree pockets. She grabbed Derek's halter and followed after the prince.

"What are you doing wandering off?" said Hetty when she caught up with him.

"I saw a frog." said Prince Cuthbert. "It was lovely and green, like a beautiful slimy emerald. I think it might be an enchanted frog. You know — a pretty girl whose been turned into a frog."

"An enchanted frog?" scoffed Penelope. "What are you planning to do with this enchanted frog? *Kiss it?*"

"Precisely," said the prince, making another grab for the hopping frog. "Come here my beauty. It's me, your handsome prince." The prince leaped onto the frog and grasped hold of it's slippery body in his hands.

"Success!" he shouted, before holding up the frog to show Hetty and Penelope. "See! She's clearly not just any *normal* frog."

The frog said, "Ribbet!" in a completely normal frog sort of way.

"It looks like any ordinary frog to me," said Hetty. "How do you know it's a pretty girl?"

"Well, she's got long eyelashes. Look!" said the prince.

Prince Cuthbert thrust the boggle-eyed creature close to Hetty's face. The frog did indeed have rather long eyelashes.

"Alright, but I don't think that necessarily means it's an enchanted frog." Hetty said.

The prince could not be swayed. He was utterly convinced that the slimy creature in his hands was an enchanted princess. He closed his eyes and puckered up his lips.

"Oh no, he's not going to..." said Penelope, covering her eyes with her wings.

"I think he is..." said Hetty, cringing.

SMMMOOOOOOCCCCCHHHHHHH!

The Prince planted a smoochy, sloppy, romantic kiss on the poor unsuspecting frog.

"Ewwww!" said Hetty. "That is really disgust—"

There was a small explosion, and a Poof of green smoke. Then, Prince Cuthbert's amour collapsed to the ground with lots of clattering and clanging. It was as if the prince had disappeared into thin air.

"What in the world?" said Hetty, tiptoeing near to the pile of silver amour and peering down at it. "Where did he go?"

Penelope crept closer, and pecked at the empty helmet. It toppled over to reveal a rather stupid looking frog.

The frog looked up at her and said, "Ribbet!"

"Prince Cuthbert?" said Penelope, hardly believing her eyes. "Is that you?"

"Ribbet! Ribbet!" said the frog.

"Oh Hetty," said Penelope. "He's only gone and turned himself into a frog!"

Prince Cuthbert, hopped over to the other frog, and sat by her side happily. "Ribbet!" he said.

And the other frog replied with a "Croak!"

This seemed to delight Prince Cuthbert. He hopped around in a circle, before settling down again next to her. The two frogs snuggled close together happily.

"I think they're... *in love*," said Hetty, astounded.

"Well, what are we going to do now?" said Penelope. "Can you change him back?"

"Oh, I never learned that spell," said Hetty. "If someone is really awful... You know, totally and utterly horrid, I have on occasion been known to turn them into a frog. But, I've never found the need to change them back..."

"I might have guessed," said Penelope. "Well, you'd better put him in your pocket then. He can stay there until we get him back home. Mervin the wizard can change him back. It's the least he could do for causing so much trouble around here."

Hetty picked up Prince Cuthbert, and tried to pop him in her front pocket. But every time she tried, he would wriggle, squiggle, and then leap out of her hands, and hop back over to his beloved new girlfriend.

"I think I will have to take them both," said Hetty. "He is clearly besotted with her."

Hetty gathered up both frogs in her hands, and then dropped them into her pocket.

"Well that's that," said Hetty. "It looks like we are facing this **dragon** on our own."

"Probably for the best," replied Penelope.

Hetty and Penelope climbed aboard Derek, and off they trekked, towards the Misty Mountain...

...And the fire breathing **dragon**.

Chapter Nine

The Misty Mountain stood a mile high, jagged and craggy, with its tallest peak hidden by clouds. Hetty, Penelope and Derek stood in awe at the bottom, craning their necks as they looked up at the towering mass of rock before them.

There was a narrow, rocky path, which spiralled around the mountain. The path led all the way up to the very top, where the **dragon** lived in her cave.

Derek bellowed with excitement. He loved climbing rocky paths. It was what he was made for. He dug at the ground with his front hoof in anticipation.

"Well at least one of us isn't terrified," clucked Penelope. "But look how high it is Hetty. It's so high there are clouds at the top!"

"I know," said Hetty. "But we made a promise to everyone that we'd try and stop the **dragon** from setting fire to everything. And a promise is a promise."

So they began their ascent, which wasn't so scary at first, but soon became steeper, and higher, and more treacherous.

The rocky path grew narrower, until Derek could hardly fit his hooves onto it as he walked.

Every now and then, a cluster of rocks would become unstuck, and tumble down the mountainside.

Hetty feel dizzy with fear.

The wind blew and whistled around them as they trudged up the crumbling path. Hetty held onto her hat with one hand so that it didn't blow away, and gripped onto the reins with the other. Penelope's strong chicken feet clutched onto Derek's fur as the gusts of wind ruffled her feathers.

As Hetty, Penelope and Derek finally got closer to the top, they became surrounded by clouds, and for a few moments Hetty almost forgot how high they were because she could no longer see the ground.

Until she remembered that clouds were usually in the SKY, and they were SO HIGH that they were IN THE CLOUDS meaning they were REALLY, REALLY HIGH UP.

Around the final bend, they finally reached the top of the mountain. It's sharp peak jutted upwards, stabbing into the grey sky. Just below the summit, they could see a dark cave. The entrance to the cave was scorched black, and puffs of grey smoke wafted out.

"I think we're here," said Hetty, with a nervous gulp.

"I am going to be turned into a roast chicken," said Penelope. "I just know it."

Hetty slid off Derek and picked up Penelope, setting her down onto the rocky ground beside her.

"Thank you, Derek," Hetty said to the surefooted llama. "That was really something."

Hetty reached into her pockets to get something nice for Derek — a piece of carrot cake perhaps. But instead, she pulled out a slimy frog. It was Prince Cuthbert. "Oops," said Hetty. "Come on Prince Cuthbert, better get you back in my pocket where you'll be safe."

Prince Cuthbert wriggled and squirmed and then jumped onto the floor. "Ribbit! Ribbet! Croak!" he said. Then he hopped away.

"Come back!" cried Hetty. "What are you doing? You can't fight a **dragon** – you're only a frog!"

But the prince didn't listen. He hop, hop, hopped his way to the entrance of the cave, and then went inside. Hetty and Penelope chased after him. "Come back!" they yelled.

Inside the cave, the huge **dragon** sat with her head facing a dark corner, fast asleep. Her long tail was curled around her body, and her huge wings were folded and still. At the sound of their footsteps behind her, she woke up and turned around. The **dragon** glared at them with fiery orange eyes.

Penelope unexpectedly popped an egg out in fright. It rolled across the cave floor.

"What are YOU doing here?" the **dragon** roared, smoke wafting from her nostrils. "How dare you disturb me in my cave when I'm sleeping. Why, I ought to sizzle you up like a couple of sausages. I ought to flame grill you like a rump steak. I ought to — OUCH!"

The **dragon** looked down, to see a small green frog, nipping at her toes ferociously. "Ouch! Get off, you pea brained pest!" she bellowed. "That's it! I'm going to frazzle you!" The **dragon** took a deep breath, preparing to blow fire at the pesky frog prince that was attacking her toes.

Hetty dashed forward. "No! Stop!" she said. "Please don't frazzle him. He's only a small helpless frog, he can't do you any harm." She gathered up the prince, and despite his wriggling, managed to shove him away into her pocket. "Get back in there, Nitwit!" she hissed under her breath.

Hetty raised her head slowly and gazed up at the humongous and very annoyed **dragon** in front of her. She cleared her throat, her voice shaking as she spoke.

"Erm, H-h-hello there, Madam D-D-**Dragon.** My name is Hetty, and I'm a witch who lives down there, in the f-f-forest. I've come to ask you, if you don't mind, would you please s-stop setting things on fire? P-p-please?"

The **dragon**'s eye's flashed with anger. "No," she replied, raising her head obstinately. "I will not."

"But why?" said Hetty. "Why won't you stop? It's causing an awful lot of bother down there."

Penelope peeked out from behind Hetty's legs. "Has something happened to make you angry? You've lived here for a long time after all, and you never used to set things on fire. At least, not so often anyway."

"I am going to keep setting the kingdom on fire, until I get my precious egg back," said the **dragon** sternly. "It was stolen from me, and I want it back."

She stomped a front foot in anger.

Penelope gasped. "Someone stole your egg! How terrible... Did it have a baby **dragon** inside?"

"It did," the **dragon** sighed. "It was almost ready to hatch. I was so excited to finally meet my little baby, and now it's gone." She hung her huge head in sorrow.

Hetty and Penelope looked at each other.

"Her egg was stolen?" said Hetty.

"You don't think?..." said Penelope.

"Well, who else could it be?" replied Hetty.

"Do *you* know who stole my egg?" said the **dragon**, her eyes widening with excitement. "Tell me who they are! Tell me where they live! I am going to burn them to a crisp! I am going to scorch them silly! I am going to reduce them to a pile of smouldering ashes!"

The **dragon** beat her great wings, preparing to fly. Huge gusts of wind blew back Hetty's hair, and Penelope's feathers.

"Wait a minute," said Hetty. "I really think it's best if we don't burn people to a crisp, unless it's *absolutely necessary*."

The **dragon** stopped beating her wings and frowned. "But how will I get my egg back?"

"Well, *I* can try to get it back for you," said Hetty. "I think I know where it is, and I think I know who stole it. All I need to do is talk to them and persuade them to return it."

"And if they refuse, *then* you can burn them to a crisp," said Penelope.

"It's a deal," said the **dragon** with a nod. "Now, would you like a lift back down the mountain? It will be much quicker than walking." She gave them her nicest smile, flashing her pearly white, pointed teeth. "You can get on my back, and I will fly you down."

"Erm... Ok then," said Hetty nervously. She really didn't relish the thought of riding on the back of a flying **dragon**. But it seemed rude to refuse such a kind offer. And it's never wise to be rude to a fire-breathing **dragon**.

Outside the cave, the **dragon** waited at the edge of the cliff for Hetty and Penelope to climb aboard her scaly back.

Before they did so, Hetty walked over to Derek. "Do you think you can make your own way back down the mountain, Derek?" she asked. "Only, I don't think you'll enjoy flying."

Derek bellowed, then spat, which Hetty took as an agreement. She gave him a piece of carrot cake, and a pat on the neck to say thank you for all his hard work. Then it was time to climb aboard the **dragon**'s back.

"Erm, Hetty..." said Penelope, as they made their way across to where the **dragon** was waiting for them. "I know I am always saying that I really hate being put into your pockets, but I think, just this once, I will go in of my own accord."

Chapter Ten

Hetty didn't like heights, or going fast, or flying. So, you could say she wasn't having the *best* time as she rode on the **dragon**'s back, high up in the sky, and flew back down the mountain as fast as a rocket.

She wrapped her arms around the **dragon**'s neck, and clung on as tight as she could, squeezing her eyes shut. "You may as well drop me off at the castle," she said, the wind whistling past her ears.

"Alright" said the **dragon**. "The castle is just over the river. Hang on tight!" She swerved to the left, and Hetty clutched on for dear life.

The dragon landed relatively gracefully for such a huge creature, with just a slight bit of turbulence and skidding, before coming to a halt by crashing into the castle door.

Hetty slid down the side of the dragon like a limp noodle, and plopped onto the ground with a groan. She then wobbled to her feet and attempted to regain her composure.

"Thank you, Dragon," she said. "That *was* much faster than walking."

"You're welcome," said the dragon. "I'll wait here, while you go and get my egg."

Hetty pulled Penelope out from her front pocket and set her down on the ground. "Well, that wasn't so bad," said the little chicken, dusting herself off. "I hardly felt a thing. We should fly by dragon more often. It *is* much quicker than walking."

"Not bloomin' likely," said Hetty. "I'm all wobbly and woozy from being up so high, and I feel a tad sick to say the least."

Hetty marched over to the castle door, and knocked on it with as much authority as she could muster. She heard a latch click, then another, then another, and the door slowly creaked open. They were greeted by a smart butler with a neat moustache and a monocle.

He looked them both up and down, with an expression on his face similar to one you might make if you'd stepped in dog's mess.

"We don't want to buy any double-glazing, thank you," he said, before closing the door again.

Hetty frowned at the closed door. And then knocked on it again.

"Oh, it's you again," said the butler.

"We need to speak to the king," said Hetty. "It's rather urgent."

"You'll have to come back later," said the butler. "The king is having a game of Wiff-Waff with Mervin the wizard."

"Wiff-Waff?" said Hetty, with a puzzled expression.

"Wiff-Waff," confirmed the butler, with a nod.

"What the tiddling tadpoles is Wiff-Waff?" said Penelope.

"It's also known as, ahem, *Ping-Pong*, amongst the common folks," the butler said, looking down his nose at the talking chicken.

"Oh," said Hetty. "Well, beg my pardon, Sir, but is the king's game of Ping-Pong more important than the imminent threat of being scorched to a crisp by a very cross **dragon**?"

"I suppose not," said the butler, looking over Hetty's shoulder at the huge green **dragon**, who was stomping up and down impatiently behind her.

"Then... Can we come in?" said Penelope.

"I suppose you'd better," he replied, and stepped aside to let them in. "I will just go and fetch His Majesty for you."

"And you can fetch that nuisance Mervin the wizard too," said Hetty, "I've got a few bones to pick with him."

"Very well," the butler said, disappearing down a corridor.

Moments later, the king arrived with Mervin the wizard. The king was wearing a white tennis outfit and a gold sweatband around his head, just under his crown. His face was red as a tomato. Mervin also wore a tennis outfit, along with his pointed wizard's hat, and had the sweatband wrapped around his long, white beard.

"Now see here," said the king, marching towards Hetty. "This better be important. I was winning!"

"It IS very important," said Hetty. "It's about the **dragon**..."

"Oh, you've killed it have you? Jolly good," said the king. "How did the boy do? I *do* hope he hasn't scuffed his brand new armour."

"Actually, the **dragon** is still very much alive," said Hetty. "And the prince is... Well, he's fine. But we'll talk about that later." Then she continued, "The **dragon** is literally fuming about her egg being stolen. So, I've come to get it back... Along with the stolen flowers from the meadow, the fairies from the forest, and the rainbow fish from the lagoon."

"I didn't steal those things," said the king. "Mervin used his magical skills to make them for me. He's very clever. He always gets me what I want."

Mervin nodded smugly in agreement.

"GREAT BIG FIBS!" clucked Penelope. "That rotten wizard stole them!"

"Did not," said Mervin.

"Did so," said Penelope.

"Mervin..." said Hetty, her voice soft and dangerous. "I think you had better tell the truth, or I shall have to put a curse on you."

"A curse – Pah! You don't scare me with your tiddly little curses," said Mervin. "You're not even that good at being a witch."

"But I *can* make your BEARD fall off," said Hetty, putting her hands on her hips. "You don't want me to do that — do you?"

Mervin's whiskers whiffled nervously. He definitely *didn't* want Hetty to make his beard fall off. He had a very weak chin.

"Alright!" he threw up his arms. "Fine. I admit it, I stole all of those things. But it is my job after all. I'm here to serve the king. And what the king *wants*, the king **gets**."

"That's right," said the king, nodding. "And I'm not giving any of it back because *I'm the king*!" He stomped his foot like a spoiled child.

"Oh yes you *are* giving it back," said Hetty sternly. "And you had better give that **dragon's egg** back right now. Or the **dragon** is going to turn this castle into a whopping great bonfire."

"But I want a pet **dragon**..." said the king, petulantly poking out his bottom lip. "The egg is nearly ready to hatch and I've got a name picked out and everything. I'm going to call him Archibald."

"**Dragons** aren't good pets, your majesty," said Hetty. "They are a very serious fire risk for a start."

"Where IS the egg?" asked Penelope. "And how on earth are you keeping it warm enough to hatch? What have you got sitting on it – an elephant?"

"Nope!" said Mervin, looking rather proud of himself. "Come and see."

Mervin led them down the corridor to the end, and opened a door. Inside, the room was filled with straw. Right in the centre of the room was a gigantic, purple and pink spotted egg. The egg had least fifty chickens sitting on the top of it.

"Chickens!" gasped Penelope. "Well... I suppose we ARE the best at incubating eggs."

"Oi!" said Hetty, suddenly remembering something. "These are Farmer Egbert's chickens! He thinks they have all been roasted alive and gobbled up by the **dragon**. You'd better give those back too!"

"Owww, do I have to?" the king whined. "It's not fair."

Hetty was just thinking that it was no wonder Prince Cuthbert had turned out the way he had with a father like this, when the giant egg began to wobble from side to side.

The chickens flapped their wings and clucked in alarm as a **jagged crack** began to appear across the top of the shell.

Chapter Eleven

The jagged crack in the huge **dragon**'s egg grew bigger, and bigger. The egg wibbled and wobbled, until all the chickens fell off the top of it. They dashed around the room flapping their wings and squawking in panic, sensing the imminent danger.

The king hopped up and down with excitement. "Come on Archibald! You can do it!" he said. "Crack open that egg! There's a good boy!"

CRACK.

CRUNCH.

CRACK.

POP!

Out popped the head of a baby **dragon**. He had large orange eyes and shiny green scales, just like his mother. The baby **dragon** hiccupped and smoke rings rose up into the air. Then he let out his very first roar.

"Awww," said the king. "Isn't he adorab—"

A jet of fire flew across the room, scorching the hair on the top of the king's head, leaving him with a smouldering bald patch.

"I did say a pet **dragon** would be a fire risk," said Hetty, ducking as another blast of fire shot just over her head.

"Make him stop Mervin!" said the king. "Make him stop!"

Mervin cracked his knuckles, and then raised his hands up into the air, saying, "Baby hatchling... Desist your flames! Arrrrggghhh!"

Another blast of scorching hot fire knocked off Mervin's hat.

"I think we'd better get out of here," said Penelope, as the baby **dragon** shook off the remainders of his eggshell, emerging fully.

Although he was only a newborn, he was about the size of a full-grown pony. The baby **dragon** began to beat his wings.

"RUN!" shouted Hetty, scooping Penelope up and diving out of the way. The baby **dragon** barged out of the open door, scattering chickens everywhere.

"Stop him!" shouted the king, as the **dragon** charged down the corridor, knocking over plinths and smashing precious vases with his long tail.

He dashed into the banquet hall, where the king kept his humongous fish tank. The tank took up the whole length of one wall, and was so tall it almost touched the ceiling. It was so big and so high, that the butler had to climb a huge ladder to sprinkle the fish food in every day.

Inside the tank, lots of fat rainbow fish floated about aimlessly. Their fins waggled from side to side, and their mouths opened and closed. The **dragon** screeched to a halt, and took a moment to admire the strange floating creatures, before letting out a roar.

He blasted the fish tank with a hot jet of flames. The heat of the fire cracked the glass. The crack grew and multiplied into more cracks. And those cracks multiplied into even more cracks, until the whole front of the tank resembled a giant spiderweb.

"My beautiful fish!" cried the king, as the tank suddenly burst, flooding the room with a tidal wave of water and bemused rainbow fish.

The water gushed down the corridor and into the hall, where it broke open the front door. The wave then carried the fish outside, sloshing across the castle gardens and leaving the fat fish flopping around on the grass. The fish flipped, and flopped, and wriggled their way into the nearby river, where they were carried away by the rapid current, all the way back home to the Blue Lagoon.

The baby **dragon**, now soggy and quite irritated, coughed and shook the water from his ears, before continuing his rampage around the castle. He burst through each door, and stampeded through every room, whipping his long tail, swooshing his wings, and blasting fire at everything in sight. Priceless statues and paintings, ancient tapestries and Persian rugs, were all scattered, smashed and scorched in the baby **dragon**'s wake.

The king grabbed hold of Mervin and shook him. "It's destroying everything!" he wailed. "DO SOMETHING!"

"There's nothing I can do!" shouted Mervin. "I've already tried! It's out of control!"

"Let him go," said Hetty. "He just wants his mother."

"Never!" replied the king. "He's mine!"

The **dragon** charged up the grand spiral staircase and stomped up and down the corridor, investigating every bedroom — apart from the queen's room where she was having a relaxing 'hot stones massage' with her therapist, Berlinda, and had locked the door.

The baby **dragon** found Prince Cuthbert the Third's bedroom and kicked down the door with his front paw. He prowled around, sniffing at the mountains of teddies, dolls and train sets which were scattered all around the place.

Then he peered curiously at the glowing string of lights which were draped all around the top of the four-poster bed in the centre of the room. Inside the little glass bulbs, tiny, glowing fairies squealed at the sight of the **dragon**, and banged their little fists on the inside of their glass prisons.

"Let us out!" they cried. "Please let us out!"

The **dragon** snorted in surprise, and then, as he turned to leave the room, his long tail snagged on the string. The fairy lights became tangled in the **dragon**'s tail and were pulled free of the bed. The little glass bulbs smashed on the floor, setting the fairies free.

"Yippee! Thanks **Dragon**!" said the fairies, and they flew away out of the open window, back home to their forest.

Sliding back down the stair banister, still soaking wet and now tangled in smashed fairy lights, the baby **dragon** hit the ground with a thud. He scrabbled his way around the polished floor until he found his footing. Then he let out an excited roar.

He'd seen what looked like an exit to the outside world, and freedom. He could see leaves, and large purple flowers, and sky. He dashed over as fast as he could, his wings flapping and his tail swooshing from side to side.

"Not the greenhouse!" yelled the king, chasing after the **dragon**. "Not the queen's collection of rare flowers!"

The **dragon** thudded into the greenhouse, only to discover that he was separated from the sky by large, clear panes of glass. He roared and stomped about, swishing his tail here and there, knocking over plant pots and spilling flowers and dirt all over the floor. Then, the baby **dragon** heard a familiar roar. He knew that roar, he'd heard it many times from inside his egg. It was his Mama!

He roared in reply, beat his wings, and flew head first into the largest window. With a huge smash, the glass pane broke into a thousand pieces, and the little **dragon** was finally free. The baby flew across the palace gardens to his mother who was waiting for him.

"Oh, come to Mama!" she cried, scooping up her precious, fiery baby in her claws and nuzzling him. "You're safe! How I've missed you, my sweet baby!"

Inside the greenhouse, the large purple flowers were now scattered all over the floor. The heavy pots which had bound them were broken into pieces, and they could finally wriggle their roots free. The tall flowers began to rise up, and walked on their roots like feet. They clambered out of the broken window, and out into the fresh air.

"Thank goodness!" the flowers said. "Now, let's get back to our meadow, and our little sproutlings!"

The king sat in a sullen heap on the floor at the bottom of the stairs looking baffled. The whole castle around him was smashed and soaking wet. Hetty walked over and sat down beside him.

“You were right,” he sighed. “**Dragons** don’t make good pets.”

Hetty nodded. “All magical creatures are best off being left where they are supposed to be.”

“Yes… I understand that now,” the king replied, with a sniffle. “I’ve been a very silly king indeed.”

Chapter Twelve

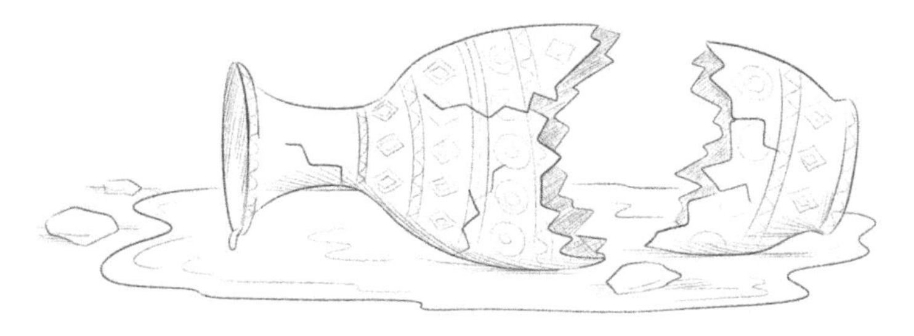

"WHAT THE DEVIL HAPPENED HERE?!" screeched the queen from the top of the stairs.

She had just finished her relaxing massage and was heading downstairs to get herself a glass of sparkling apple juice, and was confronted with the sight of her beautiful castle, all smashed to pieces and covered in puddles.

"Oh, Darling," said the king. "There's been a slight mishap."

"A slight mishap?" said the queen, slowly making her way down the stairs in a daze.

"Yes... The **dragon** egg hatched," he said. "And, it

turns out that **dragons** don't make wonderful pets at all. They are quite wild in fact. And they like *setting fire to things* — who'd have thought?"

"Everything is broken... All my priceless antiques..." the queen said, before looking around the corner at her greenhouse and shrieking. "My flowers! Where are all my rare flowers?!"

"Well, Darling, they erm, escaped," said the king, sheepishly.

The queen went all wobbly, and then fainted on the spot. A few minutes later, she opened her eyes to see a small freckle-faced witch gawping down at her, and a chicken fanning her with its wings.

"Oh my!" she said, sitting up. "It's the little Witch. You're back. Oh goodness — where is he? Where's my precious boy? He's not hurt, is he?"

"No, he's not hurt," said Hetty. "But he's not exactly *alright* either."

"Whatever do you mean?" the queen said, frowning.

"It will be best to just show you," said Hetty. "Hold out your hands, Your Majesty."

Reaching into her front dungaree pocket, Hetty rummaged around and pulled out two frogs. She knew which one was which, because the prince was distinctly more daft looking, and the other frog had long eye lashes.

She handed the daft looking frog to the queen, plopping him into her hands.

The queen shrieked.

"Eeeek! It's a slimy frog. Oh, it's hideous!" she said. "Why have you given me this horrid little frog?"

"That is your son, Your Majesty," said Hetty. "I'm afraid he accidentally turned himself into a frog by kissing this frog." She held up the other frog to show her. "I was hoping Mervin could change him back."

The queen looked stunned. "Darling?" she said, lifting the frog close to her face. "Is that really you?"

"Ribbet!" the frog replied.

"Oh, you silly, SILLY boy! Look what you've done to yourself. You're all slimy and green." Then she looked around and shouted, "Mervin! MERVIN! Get yourself out here and sort my boy out!"

Mervin appeared, sopping wet and with a scorched hat. "Yes, Your Majesty?"

She thrust the frog into his hands. "Change him back Mervin."

Mervin frowned, then a look of recognition came over his face. "Prince Cuthbert?" he said.

"Croak!" the frog replied, happily.

The wizard sighed wearily, before snapping his fingers. POOF! with a small explosion and a cloud of green smoke, Prince Cuthbert returned back to his human form.

He stood there looking bemused, wearing nothing but his polka dot boxer shorts. The queen scuttled away for a moment and came back with a velvet dressing gown to protect his modesty.

"Ribbet!" he said, "Oh gosh, beg your pardon.
I mean, thank you, Mervin."

"You're welcome, Sir," replied Mervin.

"What have I told you about kissing frogs?" the queen said crossly. "It's no way to find a princess, my love. It only works in fairy tales."

"Oh, but Mummy I *have* found a princess!" said the prince, scooping up the frog from Hetty's hands. "She's here! My princess! Isn't she simply divine?"

"Darling... That's not a princess. It's a frog," replied the queen, as gently as she could.

The prince turned to Mervin and tugged on his beard, "Oh Mervin, can you change her into a human? Can you? Can you? Can you please?"

Mervin shook his head. "Your Highness, I *could* turn this frog into a human, but you see, it just wouldn't really work."

"But why?" said the prince, looking sullen.

"Because, Your Majesty, when YOU were changed into a frog, by whatever enchantment was placed on this animal, YOU still had your human thoughts and feelings, because that was your original form... Do you follow?"

"Yeeees?" said the Prince, pretending he understood.

"And, you see the issue is, this frog — is a FROG." Mervin continued. "And if we change it into a human, it will still keep it's original FROGGY thoughts and feelings."

The prince blinked. "I don't see the issue, Mervin."

"Oh Mervin!" cried the King impatiently. "You are the laziest wizard I've ever had the displeasure of employing. Just do what the boy wants! Change his frog into a princess at once!"

Mervin sighed, "As you wish, Your Majesty."

He clicked his fingers, and with a POOF! and a POP! and a cloud of green smoke, the small frog was transformed into a pretty lady wearing a frilly green dress. She had long green hair, green eyes, and fluttery eye lashes.

"My DARLING!" the prince cried, dashing over to her and gathering her in his arms romantically.

"Ribbet!" said the princess. "Croak! Ribbet!" She wriggled out of the prince's grasp, crouched down on all fours, and began to hop and leap around the room.

"What on EARTH is she doing?" screeched the queen in shock.

"I did try to explain," said Mervin. "She is a FROG which has been changed into a human form. Therefore, she is still a FROG inside her brain..." he sighed. "I did try to tell you. It never works well this way around, Maam."

"Ohh," said the queen, finally understanding. "Oh dear. Well, I suppose you'd better change her back then."

"NO!" shouted Prince Cuthbert, standing bravely in front of the princess and shielding her. "You can't change her back! I love her, and I think she's perfect and I'm going to marry her!"

"Ribbet!" said the princess, hopping her way into the banquet hall, and then sitting down in a nice wet puddle. Prince Cuthbert smiled at her adoringly, like she was the most wonderful thing in the entire world.

The king sidled up next to the queen and put his arm around her, "Darling? Who are we to tell him who to fall in love with? Hmm?" He gave her a squeeze. "After all, don't you remember how we met?"

"I do," she said wistfully. "Those glass slippers gave me terrible blisters."

Hetty looked on and sighed contentedly. "Well, Penelope, I'd say our work here is done — wouldn't you?"

"Oh yes. A job well done," replied Penelope. "Now, can we please go back home and put the kettle on? I'm gasping for a cup of tea."

"Of course," said Hetty. "I was just going to say the same myself."

The End

In case you were wondering whether Derek made it down the mountain safely, don't panic — he's absolutely fine.

He *did* decide to stay up there for a little while longer to enjoy the fresh mountain air and spend some time exploring all the treacherous rocky paths.

I'm sure he will make his way back home eventually.

About the Author

Zoe Saunders

When she's not illustrating books for other authors, Zoe is writing and illustrating her own.

She also enjoys baking cakes (and eating them), gardening, reading, talking to her chickens, and laughing at her own jokes — much to the dismay of her long-suffering husband.

You can catch up with Zoe via her website:

www.whimsicolourart.com

Ingram Content Group UK Ltd.
Milton Keynes UK
UKHW012011100423
419951UK00002B/27